HENRY HECKELBECK

Spy vs. Spy

By **Wanda Coven**

Illustrated by **Priscilla Burris**

LITTLE SIMON
New York   London   Toronto   Sydney   New Delhi

LITTLE SIMON
An imprint of Simon & Schuster Children's Publishing Division
1230 Avenue of the Americas, New York, New York 10020
First Little Simon hardcover edition September 2021
Copyright © 2021 by Simon & Schuster, Inc.
Also available in a Little Simon paperback edition.
All rights reserved, including the right of reproduction in whole or in part in any form. LITTLE SIMON is a registered trademark of Simon & Schuster, Inc., and associated colophon is a trademark of Simon & Schuster, Inc.
For information about special discounts for bulk purchases, please contact Simon & Schuster Special Sales at 1-866-506-1949 or business@simonandschuster.com. The Simon & Schuster Speakers Bureau can bring authors to your live event. For more information or to book an event contact the Simon & Schuster Speakers Bureau at 1-866-248-3049 or visit our website at www.simonspeakers.com.
Designed by Leslie Mechanic
Manufactured in the United States of America 0821 FFG
10 9 8 7 6 5 4 3 2 1
This book has been cataloged with the Library of Congress.
ISBN 978-1-5344-8637-9 (hc)
ISBN 978-1-5344-8636-2 (pbk)
ISBN 978-1-5344-8638-6 (eBook)

CONTENTS

Chapter 1

Henry Heckelbeck spied a new mystery behind the playground swing set.

"What's THAT?" he asked.

His best friend, Dudley Day, zoomed in on the object.

"My spy sense tells me it's personal property," he said. The boys crept closer.

Henry smiled. "Well, my spy sense tells me its somebody's LUNCH BOX!"

Dudley put a finger to his lips. "Shh, not so loud. Remember Spy Rule Number Five!"

Henry covered his mouth with his hand. "Oops, sorry!" he whispered. "Spy Rule Number Five: A spy never calls attention to themselves."

 The boys crouched over the dark purple lunch box.

"Don't touch it," Henry warned.

"Why not?" Dudley asked.

"Because the owner might be watching!" Henry told him.

Dudley looked around. School was over, and the playground was nearly empty.

"I doubt it," said Dudley. "There's hardly anyone over here."

Henry scanned the playground. He motioned to a couple of third graders on the monkey bars and some kids playing four square.

Dudley saw them too. But he wasn't worried. "They're so far away that they're practically in the next town!" he said.

Henry gave a big shrug and reminded his friend that a spy can never be too careful.

Then Henry pulled out a magnifying glass.

He always carried one just in case. He held the magnifying glass over the top of the lunch box.

"Dancing robots," Henry noted.

Dudley corrected Henry. "No, those are BATTLING robots."

Henry looked again. "Could be," he said. "But if it's dancing robots, this lunch box belongs to Nina Noff. Remember when she brought her Boogie Bot to school?"

"Oh yeah," Dudley said with a laugh. "It was taken away because of the no-toys-at-school rule. Did Nina ever get her Boogie Bot back?"

Henry nodded. "Yup, but I heard she almost got it taken away again on the bus ride home because it started singing in her backpack!"

The boys cracked up. Then they got right back into spy mode.

"Well, if the robots on the lunch box are BATTLING, then the lunch box probably belongs to Ryan Riley," said Dudley. "He always doodles battling robots."

The boys kept their eyes fixed on the lunch box.

"I wish we could open it," said Henry.

Dudley nodded. "Me too, but it might be a trap."

Henry stroked his chin thoughtfully. "We need to think like super spies!"

Chapter 2

A LITTLE LUCK

Henry had an idea.

"I've got it!" said Henry. "A super spy would use x-ray glasses. Then we could see what's inside the lunch box without opening it."

"But we don't have x-ray glasses," Dudley said with a sigh. "Maybe we just need some good luck. Let's find a lost penny!"

The boys searched around for good-luck pennies.

They couldn't find one.

"How about a four-leaf clover?" Dudley suggested.

Henry glanced across the huge lawn beside the playground and whistled. "That's too much work."

Then Dudley craned his head toward the sky and said, "Maybe a bird will poop on us! I've heard bird poop is REALLY good luck."

Henry wrinkled his nose. "That's gross."

Both boys laughed.

Then they heard clattering behind them on the path. It was getting closer. They whipped around to see what was up.

It was a girl on a scooter,
and she was moving fast!

"Look out!" she yelled.

The boys dove onto the grass.
CRASH! The scooter rammed
into the lunch box, and the
girl rolled safely onto the soft
ground. She hopped up and
dusted herself off.

"Are you OKAY?"
asked Henry.

The girl grabbed
her scooter as if
nothing big had happened.

"YUP!" she cheered. "Thanks for getting out of the way!"

Then she rode off without looking back.

The boys shrugged to each other, then ran to the lunch box. It had burst open in the crash.

"It's a MIRACLE!" cried Dudley. "And we didn't even have to get pooped on by a bird!"

Henry shoved Dudley as a joke before looking at the lunch box clues. There was an empty bag of pretzels.

"Who eats pretzels?" Henry asked.

"Um, lots of kids," Dudley answered as he picked up half a sandwich with two bites missing. "But who doesn't finish a hummus and veggie sandwich?"

Dudley held the half-eaten
sandwich in front of Henry's
face. It smelled kind of yummy.

"Nobody *I* know!" Henry
said.

Dudley agreed and dropped
the sandwich back into the
lunch box.

The boys looked for more clues. They found a brown apple core on the ground next to a rainbow water bottle that was rolling away from the scene.

"Our clue is making a getaway!" Henry called out.

The friends both leaped for it. But somebody else got to it first.

It was a fellow spy, Max Maplethorpe.

Chapter 3

TOP SPY

"What are you doing to that POOR lunch box?" asked Max as she picked up the water bottle.

The boys looked at each other and then back at Max.

They thought she'd gone home.

"It wasn't US," said Henry. "A girl ran over the lunch box with her scooter."

"And what are you doing with our clue?" cried Dudley. He reached for the water bottle, but Max slipped it inside her jacket.

Henry jumped forward. "Wait!" he cried. "That water bottle could have fingerprints on it to help us solve the mystery of the lunch box!"

Max folded her arms over her jacket, where she had the water bottle.

"A clue AND a mystery?" she asked. "Are you guys spying WITHOUT me?"

Henry threw his hands up in the air.

"Well, not on PURPOSE!"
he said. "We just happened to
stumble on the lunch box!"

Dudley nodded. "And all we
want to do is return it to its
rightful owner."

Max pulled the water bottle from her jacket. "Have you figured out who it belongs to?" she asked.

Henry stared at Dudley because they hadn't solved the mystery yet.

"Well," he said, "*I* think the lunch box belongs to Nina Noff, because she likes dancing robots."

Dudley pointed to the lid on the lunch box so Max could see the robots. "And I see battling robots," said Dudley. "That means it probably belongs to Ryan Riley."

Meanwhile, Henry picked up a stick and poked the rotten apple core on the ground.

"Hold on!" he exclaimed. "Ryan never ever eats whole apples after he found out worms could live INSIDE apples. Now he only eats sliced ones."

"Whoa, you're right!" said Dudley. "And that means the lunch box belongs to Nina Noff. Case CLOSED."

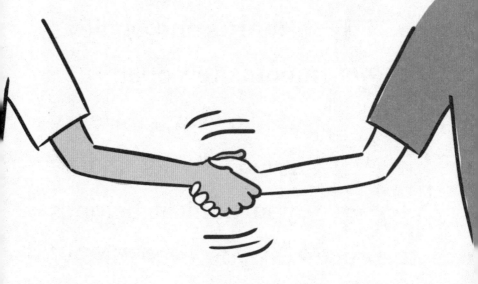

Dudley held out his hand, and Henry shook it.

"Not so fast, guys!" said Max. "Because you're BOTH wrong. This lunch box belongs to Bruce Bickerson."

Henry's and Dudley's mouths fell open.

"No way!" Henry cried. "What makes you think it belongs to Bruce? Do you even KNOW him?"

Max shook her head.

"Nope," she said, "but if you guys were really GOOD spies, you would've noticed his name written on this water bottle."

Max held it up, and on the side it read BRUCE BICKERSON in black marker.

"So NOW who's the BEST spy in town?" Max asked with a sly smile.

Chapter 4

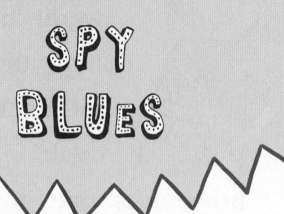

SPY BLUES

Henry slammed the back door shut, stomped into the kitchen, and dropped the mystery lunch box onto the kitchen table.

His older sister, Heidi, was sitting there doing homework.

"What in the world are you doing with Bruce's robot lunch box?" she asked.

Bruce was one of Heidi's best friends.

"He left it on the playground," Henry said with a huff. "Would you give it back to him?"

Heidi nodded. "Sure."

She continued to stare at her little brother. He had a long face and droopy shoulders.

"Okay, what's wrong?" she asked.

Henry slumped onto a chair across from Heidi.

"It's just . . . ," he started. "Am I a good spy?"

Heidi tapped her pencil eraser on her math book.

"Well, let's see," she said. "You're SMART. You spot things other people don't see. And you love mysteries. I'm pretty sure that makes you an amazing spy."

Henry propped his elbows on the table and rested his chin in his hands. "Are you just saying that because you're my SISTER?"

Heidi shook her head. "Nope. Why?"

Henry shrugged and said, "I had a bad spy day—that's all." Heidi stuck out her lower lip.

"Well, everybody has an off day once in a while," she admitted. "Even me."

A small smile turned at the corner of Henry's mouth. "Aww, you're just being nice."

Heidi laughed. "Trust me, I don't HAVE to be nice! That's Mom and Dad's job. You're just a good spy."

Now Henry let out a real smile because he knew his sister was telling the truth. "Thanks, Sis."

Chapter 5

THE SUPER SPIES

At school the next day Henry, Dudley, and Max were in the same math group.

Ms. Mizzle gave each group a different word problem that they had to solve.

When the group got the answer right, they earned a point for their team.

They had named themselves the Super Spies. Henry read their group's word problem out loud.

"Jamie has two apples and four grapes. Lee has ten grapes and three oranges. Curtis has five mangoes. How much fruit do they have altogether?"

Part of being in a group meant that they had to work as a team.

Since Dudley had the best pencil, they decided he should start the answer.

"Jamie has six pieces of fruit," said Dudley.

He wrote the number six on a piece of paper and handed it to Henry.

"And Lee has thirteen pieces of fruit." Henry wrote a plus sign after the number six, followed by the number thirteen.

6 + 13

"And poor ol' Curtis only has five mangoes," said Max. She added another plus sign, followed by the number five. "Now we have to add them all up."

Max stacked the equation to make it easier to add the numbers. Then she drew a line underneath them.

"Six plus three equals nine," she said. "Your turn, Henry."

Henry put his hand under the table and counted on his fingers.

"And nine plus five equals fourteen," he announced.

He wrote down the four and carried the one.

$$\begin{array}{r} {}^{1}6 \\ 13 \\ + 5 \\ \hline 4 \end{array}$$

"And one plus one is TWO," said Max. "And that makes a total of . . ."

"Twenty-four!" they all said at the same time.

Ms. Mizzle came over and checked the answer.

"Well done," she said. "That's one point for the Super Spies. Now here's an extra-credit question: How can the fruit be split up evenly among the three friends?"

Max swiped their answer sheet and slid it in front of her. "Since I'm the BEST spy on the team, I'll solve the extra-credit question."

Dudley slapped his hand on the table. "Hey, that's not true!" he said angrily. "Henry and I are MAJOR spies! You just got lucky yesterday. Right, Henry?"

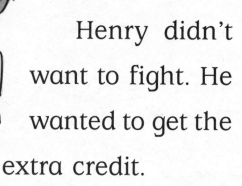

Henry didn't want to fight. He wanted to get the extra credit.

"Come on, team," he said. "Let's just solve the problem together."

Max shook her head. "I have an even better idea," she said. "Let's each solve the problem on our own. That way we'll know who's truly the best spy."

Henry rolled his eyes and pointed out that this was a *math* problem. It had nothing to do with *spying*.

Then Max leaned across the desk. "Sounds like you're afraid of LOSING again, Henry."

"You know what, Max?"
Henry said. "We should have
a real SPY CONTEST and
settle this once and for all. I
mean, unless you're chicken.
Bawk-bawk."

"Oh, it's on!" Max said without blinking.

Dudley pumped his fist and cheered. "YES! We can start at lunch. Whoever spies the coolest stuff WINS."

Henry's and Max's eyes were still locked.

"May the BEST spy win," said Henry.

Max smirked. "And the best spy will be ME."

"No, ME!" challenged Henry.

"Hey, what about ME?" said Dudley.

And that was how the Super Spies turned on one another.

Chapter 6

GAME ON

The three spies met at recess with their notebooks.

"Spy contest rules," Henry began. "Rule Number One: You cannot get caught. If anybody sees you—you're out."

Max and Dudley took notes.
Henry continued, "Okay,
Rule Number Two: You only
write down COOL stuff you
spy. Boring, everyday stuff
doesn't count. Got it?"

The others nodded.

"Now it's GAME ON!" Henry cried. The spies each went in a different direction.

Henry peered into his classroom window. The room was empty. He scanned the classroom for something cool. He was about to give up when he spotted Nina Noff's Boogie Bot in her cubby.

Henry wrote in his notebook. *Nina brought her Boogie Bot BACK to school! That's a secret worth knowing!*

Then he went to the cafeteria window and peeked inside. He spied the kitchen workers eating lunch. Henry gasped.

No way! The workers eat the SAME food as US! Henry jotted this find in his notebook too.

Then he ran back onto the playground. There he spied two boys trading pens. He also spied a girl who let a tiny Super Ball go at the top of the swirly slide.

Round and round it went until it bounced onto the ground.

That was awesome! Henry thought as he scribbled this and more notes down in his notebook.

Then someone tapped Henry on the shoulder. Henry jumped. It was Principal Pennypacker.

"I didn't mean to startle you, Henry!" the principal said.

Henry closed his notebook and tried to act normal. "Uh, that's okay. What's up?"

Principal Pennypacker gave a smile and asked, "Have you seen Ryan Riley anywhere? I have a message from his mom."

Henry's shoulders relaxed. *I'm safe,* he thought as he looked around for Ryan. He spotted him at the top of the slide. Then he noticed that Dudley was hiding under the slide, taking notes.

"Ryan's on the slide," Henry said, pointing. "But don't pay any attention to Dudley under the slide, okay?"

Principal Pennypacker laughed. "Okay, then. I'll ignore Dudley. Thanks for your help."

Henry watched nervously as the principal walked toward Dudley. Had he just ruined the game for his friend?

Then Ryan Riley went down the slide and landed right next to Dudley.

"What are you writing in that notebook, Dudley?" Ryan yelled so the whole playground could hear.

Oh no! Henry thought. *Dudley's been caught! Spying is a dangerous game!*

Chapter 7

THE WINNER IS . . . !

The three spies met up after school. It was time for them to compare notes.

"I hear that Dudley's O-U-T— OUT," said Max.

Dudley looked at the ground.

"And I was SO close to finding out who's been picking flowers in our class garden!" he said.

Max shrugged. "Well, CLOSE doesn't win contests."

Henry patted Dudley on the back. "Sorry, Dudster."

Dudley shrugged it off. "Oh well, let's find out the winner. Henry, you go first."

Henry opened his notebook and read his spy notes. He had twelve of them.

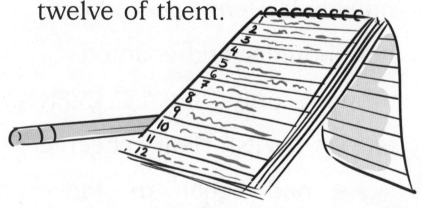

"Great spying, Henry!" said Dudley. "Your turn, Max."

When she opened her notebook, Henry peeked over her shoulder and counted.

"Max only has ELEVEN entries! I WIN!" Henry cheered and began to dance around. "Now who's the BEST spy in town?"

Max waited for Henry to stop bopping around. "Are you DONE?" she asked calmly.

Henry pushed his chest out. "Maybe. WHY?"

Max held her notebook in front of Henry and turned the page. Henry saw another entry.

Number 12: Spied Principal Pennypacker looking for Ryan.

Henry's face turned red. "HEY, THAT'S NO FAIR! I knew that TOO! I just didn't write it down!"

Max shook her head. "Well, it doesn't matter, because you didn't SPY on the principal. He came up and ASKED if you had seen Ryan. But I actually OVERHEARD him . . . like a SPY."

Henry looked to Dudley for help.

"She's right," said Dudley. "That makes the contest a TIE."

Henry groaned. "But who wants to TIE for BEST SPY?"

Max shoved her notebook into her back pocket. "NOT ME," she said. "We need a TIEBREAKER."

Dudley held up a finger.

"And I have the perfect tiebreaker game!" he said. "Anyone up for a round of What's Missing?"

Chapter 8

WHAT'S MISSING?

Dudley went over the rules for What's Missing?

"Each player gets five minutes in the other player's room. The player only takes ONE thing from the room.

If the other player figures out
WHAT'S MISSING, they win.
Got it?"

Henry and Max nodded.

Then Henry added some
more rules. "Players can only
take something in plain sight.

No opening drawers
or closets. Players
also have to give the
object back, no matter what."

Max gave a thumbs-up. "So,
where do we start?"

"Henry's house," said Dudley.

The spies headed to Henry's home. Nobody said a word the whole way. When they got there, they went straight to his bedroom.

"Okay, you've got FIVE minutes," Henry told Max. "And good luck fooling me. I know every inch of my room by heart."

"We'll see," she said as she opened the door and disappeared inside.

Dudley set a timer on his watch. Henry paced down the hallway. He wondered what Max would take.

Would she take one of his dragon action figures? Or his pirate sword?

Suddenly Henry thought of something worse. *Oh no!* he thought. *What if she takes my MAGIC BOOK?*

Henry ran to his door, but Dudley blocked the way. "You know the rules!" Dudley said. "No spying on the spy!"

 Henry raked his hand through his hair. His whole body began to shake. If Max found his book, then she'd definitely find out his wizarding secret.

Finally the door to his room opened. Max walked out with something hidden behind her back. She had a total know-it-all look on her face.

"I've really got you THIS time, Henry Heckelbeck," she said. "Your secret's NOT safe with me."

Chapter 9

SPY MAGIC

Henry raced into his room. His mind was filled with questions. *Why did Max have that weird look on her face? Does she know ALL my secrets? Did she TAKE my magic book?*

Henry ran to his bookshelf and cupped his hand over his mouth. His magic book was gone! He sat on his bed and tried to calm down.

Maybe I left it somewhere else, he wondered.

Henry began to
search his room. He
looked in drawers,
under his bed, and
in the closet—even
though those
places were off-
limits in the
game. But it didn't

matter. The book
was nowhere to
be found.

Then Henry remembered his magic book always came to him in times of need.

Maybe if I wish hard enough, my book will come back, he thought.

Henry shut his eyes and made a wish, but the book did not appear.

What would happen if Max
and Dudley found out about
Henry's magic? Would they
still be his friends? Could it
make the magic stop working?

Dudley poked his
head in the room
and announced,
"Time's up!"

Then he and
Max both walked
into the bedroom.

Max still had her hands hidden behind her back.

"Okay, Mr. Super Spy," she said. "Guess what's missing."

Henry looked around his room one more time.

How do I ask a spy if she stole my secret magic book? he wondered.

Then Henry noticed a tiny
glowing light in the hallway
behind the others. It was
his magic book! The book
hovered in the air as if to say,
Everything is okay.

Max stared at Henry.

"What are you looking at?" she asked as she turned around only to see an empty hallway.

The magic book had vanished again.

"Nothing," said Henry. "Which is just like what's missing from my room. My spy sense tells me that you took . . . absolutely nothing."

Chapter 10

THE BEST SPY

Max whipped her hands out from behind her back.

She held her fists in front of Henry and slowly opened them.

Her palms were empty.

"How did you KNOW?" Dudley cheered.

Henry laughed. "A spy will never tell."

Max put her hands on her hips. "Oh, come on! Just tell me! Do you have a spy camera in here?"

Henry laughed. "No way! I knew you'd try to outsmart me, because you're a great spy. And I couldn't find anything missing from my room— so I guessed you didn't take anything."

Dudley held up Henry's hand. "We have a winner!"

Henry pulled his arm down. "But the game isn't over! We still have to go to Max's house for round two!"

Max shook her head. "No, thanks," she said. "You win, because there's NO WAY I'm letting you into my room alone."

Henry wished he'd thought of that before.

"You're right," he agreed. "Spies should never let other spies go into their rooms. Let's call it a draw."

Max nodded. "Sounds good to me!"

Dudley clapped loudly. "Then it's settled," he said. "We're ALL the best spies! Now it's time for a new mission. Who wants to go spy on Henry's dad and see what new flavor of soda he's working on?"

"Game on!" said Henry and
Max at the same time.

And just like that, the Super
Spies were back on the case.

Check out the next book starring

Henry Heckelbeck was thrilled because it was Friday. And Friday meant no homework until Monday. *Woooo!*

Then his teacher, Ms. Mizzle, made an announcement.

An excerpt from *Henry Heckelbeck Builds a Robot*

She said, "Class, I'm assigning a very *special* science project!"

Henry looked over at his best friend, Dudley Day. Both boys knew "special project" meant "homework." And they were both right.

Ms. Mizzle smiled. "I think you'll like this one. We are going to build robots!"

The class gasped, and

everyone began talking until Ms. Mizzle whistled through her fingers. The class buzz stopped.

"You have one week to build your robot," she said.

"Can we make the robot however we want?" asked Adia Ackers.

Ms. Mizzle nodded. "Yes! Use any materials you'd like. Have fun! Be creative!"

An excerpt from *Henry Heckelbeck Builds a Robot*